BIGGEST SUPER BOWL PLAYS

by Paul Bowker

12 STORY LIBRARY

www.12StoryLibrary.com

12-Story Library is an imprint of Bookstaves.

Photographs ©: Peter Read Miller/Associated Press, cover, 1; NFL/Associated Press, 4; Staff Sgt. Bradley Lail/US Air Force, 5; charnsitr/Shutterstock.com, 5; Tony Tomsic/Associated Press, 6; dean bertoncelj/Shutterstock.com, 7; Al Messerschmidt/Associated Press, 8; PD, 9; Carol M. Highsmith/Library of Congress, 9; Tony Tomsic/Associated Press, 10; Everett Collection/Shutterstock.com, 11; Al Messerschmidt/Associated Press, 12; swimfinfan/CC2.0, 13; Phil Sandlin/Associated Press, 14; Chris O'Meara/Associated Press, 15; John Gaps III/Associated Press, 16; PD, 17; Kathy Willens/Associated Press, 18; charnsitr/Shutterstock.com, 19; Charlie Riedel/Associated Press, 20; Matt Slocum/Associated Press, 22; ncbronte/CC2.0, 23; John Bazemore/Associated Press, 24; Charlie Riedel/Associated Press, 25; Peter Read Miller/Associated Press, 26; Jeffrey Beall/CC3.0, 27; meunierd/Shutterstock.com, 28; neftali/Shutterstock.com, 28; Charlie Riedel/Associated Press, 29

ISBN
978-1-63235-546-1 (hardcover)
978-1-63235-664-2 (ebook)

Library of Congress Control Number: 2018948078

Printed in the United States of America
Mankato, MN
June 2018

12 STORY LIBRARY

Access free, up-to-date content on this topic plus a full digital version of this book. Scan the QR code on page 31 or use your school's login at 12StoryLibrary.com.

Table of Contents

1

Super Bowl X: Swann Makes a Leaping Catch

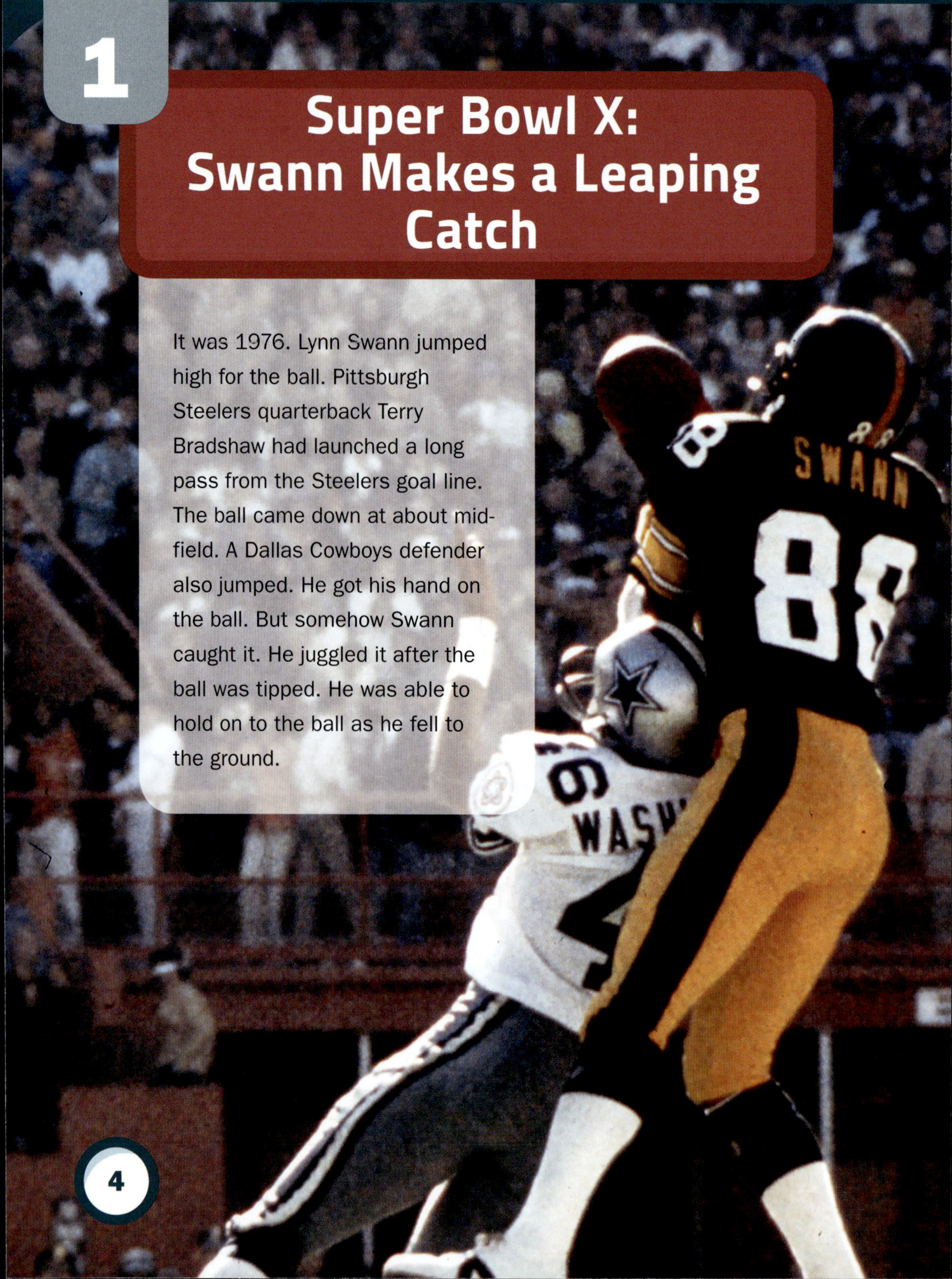

It was 1976. Lynn Swann jumped high for the ball. Pittsburgh Steelers quarterback Terry Bradshaw had launched a long pass from the Steelers goal line. The ball came down at about mid-field. A Dallas Cowboys defender also jumped. He got his hand on the ball. But somehow Swann caught it. He juggled it after the ball was tipped. He was able to hold on to the ball as he fell to the ground.

The catch by Swann in just the tenth Super Bowl game became known as a classic play. It did not score a touchdown. Lynn Swann later said he wished he had caught the ball cleanly and run for a touchdown.

Swann had four catches for 161 yards and one touchdown. He was named Super Bowl MVP.

364

Receiving yards by Lynn Swann in four Super Bowl games for the Pittsburgh Steelers.

- The juggling catch by Swann in Super Bowl X is considered to be one of the best catches in Super Bowl history.
- Swann caught four passes for 161 yards and one touchdown. He was named MVP.
- Swann was inducted into the Pro Football Hall of Fame in 2001.

ALMOST MISSED OUT

Lynn Swann almost didn't play in Super Bowl X for the Pittsburgh Steelers. He was knocked out and sustained a concussion in the American Football Conference championship game. He was hit by George Atkinson of the Oakland Raiders. He spent two days in a hospital. Swann was able to recover in time to play in the Super Bowl.

2

Super Bowl XIII: Stallworth Is a Catching Machine

John Stallworth already had scored one touchdown in Super Bowl XIII, in 1979. He was not finished.

Stallworth was a receiver for the Pittsburgh Steelers. He ran deep on a pass route in the second quarter of Super Bowl XIII. He caught the pass from Steelers quarterback Terry Bradshaw. A defender for the Dallas Cowboys tried to make a play. He fell to the ground. Stallworth kept running. Stallworth scored on the play that covered 75 yards. It was

268

Receiving yards in four Super Bowl games by Pittsburgh Steelers John Stallworth.

- Stallworth tied a Super Bowl record in Super Bowl XIII with a touchdown catch covering 75 yards.
- He caught three passes for 115 yards in the first half of Super Bowl XIII. The Steelers defeated the Dallas Cowboys.
- Stallworth helped the Steelers win the Super Bowl four times.
- He was inducted into the Pro Football Hall of Fame in 2002.

tied for the longest touchdown pass in Super Bowl history.

Stallworth had three catches in the first half alone for the Steelers. They totaled 115 yards.

The Steelers defeated the Cowboys by a score of 35 to 31. Stallworth and teammate Lynn Swann helped the Steelers win their third Super Bowl in five years.

Stallworth came through again for the Steelers one year later in Super Bowl XIV. He combined with Bradshaw on a touchdown pass covering 73 yards. He had another catch for 45 yards that set up another touchdown. Steelers won their fourth Super Bowl.

3

Super Bowl XVII: Riggins Runs for a Record

The Washington Redskins trailed the Miami Dolphins by four points. It was the fourth quarter of Super Bowl XVII, 1983. The Redskins were facing fourth down. They were at the Miami 43-yard line. They did not try for a field goal. Instead, the Redskins called a play for running back John Riggins. His power running was so strong that he was known as The Diesel.

Riggins got the ball. He was hit at the line of scrimmage by Dolphins

230

Rushing yards by John Riggins in two Super Bowl games for the Washington Redskins.

- Riggins ran 43 yards for a touchdown on a fourth-down play in Super Bowl XVII.
- He set a Super Bowl record by rushing 166 yards. He was named game MVP.
- Riggins helped the Redskins defeat the Miami Dolphins by a score of 27 to 17.

MISSED THE PARADE

John Riggins was the MVP of Super Bowl XVII. He missed the Washington Redskins victory parade because he forgot to change his watch. The game was played in Pasadena, California. Pasadena is on Pacific Coast time. He did not change his watch back to Eastern time when he returned to Washington D.C. When he woke up at 9 a.m. it was actually noon.

cornerback Don McNeal. The hit was not big enough. Riggins bounced off McNeal. He stayed on his feet. Riggins headed for the sidelines and kept running. He ran all the way for a touchdown.

The play gave the Redskins the lead by three points. They scored another touchdown later in the fourth quarter. The Redskins defeated the Dolphins by a score of 27 to 17.

Riggins was named Super Bowl MVP. He ran for a Super Bowl record 166 yards. He had 38 rushing attempts. That was also a Super Bowl record.

4

Super Bowl XVIII: Allen Reverses a Play

Marcus Allen found himself trapped after taking a handoff from Los Angeles Raiders quarterback Jim Plunkett. It was Super Bowl XVIII in 1984. Washington Redskins safety Ken Coffey was ready to make the tackle. Allen spun the play away from Coffey. He took the running play in the opposite direction and turned it into a record touchdown run. Allen broke the play 74 yards for a touchdown. It was the longest touchdown run in Super Bowl history.

The run by Allen became one of the most iconic plays in Raiders history. It was the longest run of his NFL career. It was a power run to the left side of the offensive line. Right guard Mickey Marvin was to clear the way for Allen. It didn't work out that way. So Allen turned it downfield on the right side.

The record run was a part of a big day for Allen and the Raiders. Allen rushed for 191 yards. That was also a Super Bowl record. He scored two touchdowns. The Raiders defeated the Redskins by a score of 38 to 9. Allen was named Super Bowl MVP.

The record stood until Willie Parker of the Pittsburgh Steelers scored on a run of seventy-five yards in Super Bowl XL.

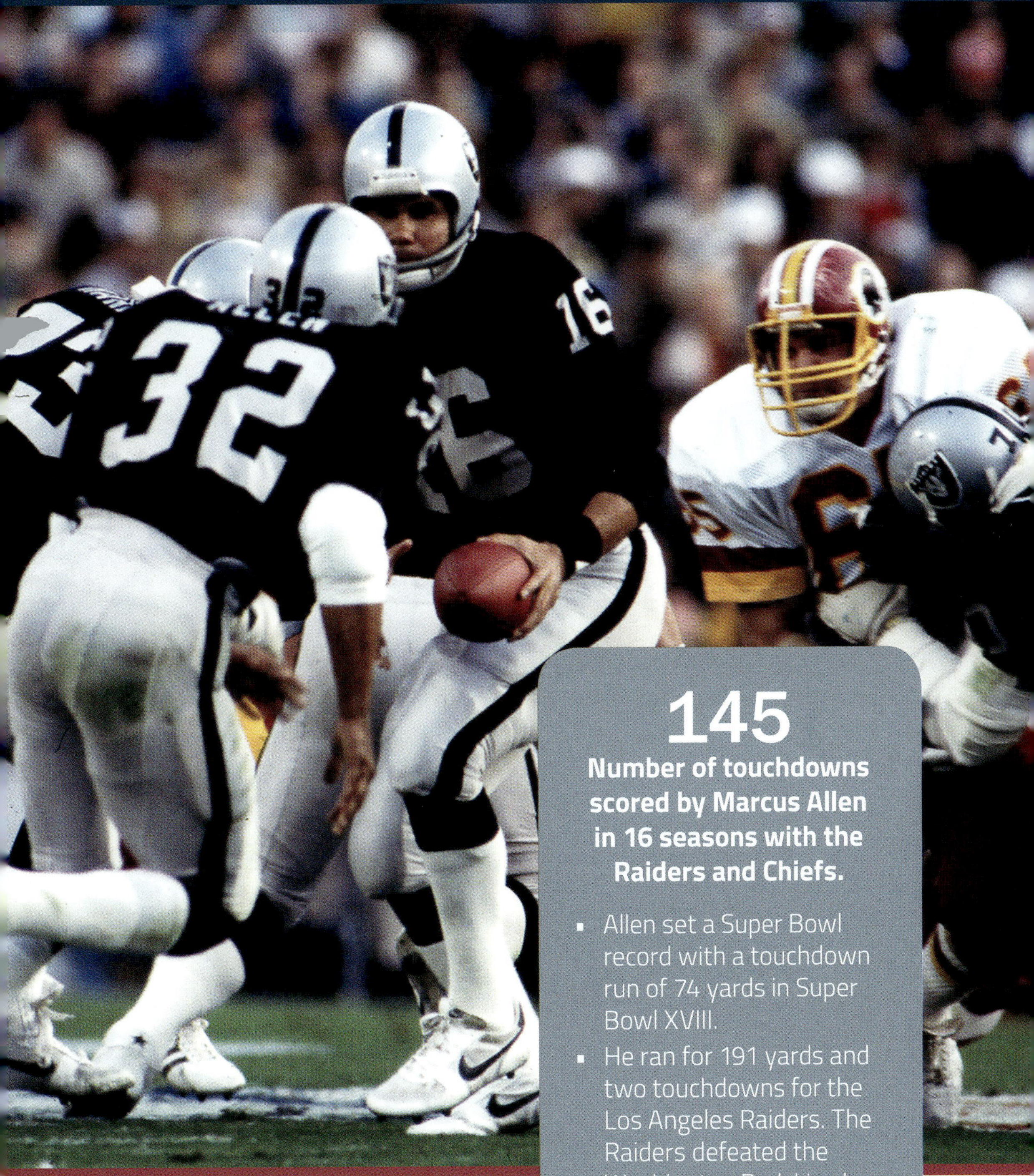

145

Number of touchdowns scored by Marcus Allen in 16 seasons with the Raiders and Chiefs.

- Allen set a Super Bowl record with a touchdown run of 74 yards in Super Bowl XVIII.
- He ran for 191 yards and two touchdowns for the Los Angeles Raiders. The Raiders defeated the Washington Redskins by a score of 38 to 9.
- Allen was named Super Bowl MVP.

5 Super Bowl XXIII: Taylor Catches a Winning Pass

Less than four minutes remained in Super Bowl XXIII of 1989. The San Francisco 49ers trailed the Cincinnati Bengals by a score of 16 to 13. They were at their own 8-yard line. John Taylor had no idea he was about to catch the winning touchdown pass in a Super Bowl. He had not caught any passes in the game.

Quarterback Joe Montana led the 49ers on a touchdown drive of 92 yards. Taylor caught a touchdown pass covering 10 yards from Montana. It came with just 34 seconds left in the game. It gave the 49ers a victory by a score of 20 to 16.

The scoring pass concluded a drive that consisted of several big plays. Montana completed a pass of 27 yards to Jerry Rice. That play gave the 49ers the ball at the Bengals 18-yard line. Taylor scored two plays later.

1

Number of catches by John Taylor in Super Bowl XXIII.

- Taylor caught a touchdown pass from Joe Montana with 34 seconds left. The play produced a 20-16 win for the 49ers against the Cincinnati Bengals.
- The touchdown pass finished off a scoring drive of 92 yards in the final minutes of the game.
- It was the third Super Bowl victory for Montana. He won another Super Bowl ring in Super Bowl XXIV.

UNBEATEN CHAMP

Joe Montana never lost a Super Bowl game. He won four Super Bowls as quarterback of the San Francisco 49ers. He was named MVP twice. In one Super Bowl when he was not MVP, Montana threw a winning touchdown pass in the final minute. He was the first quarterback to win four Super Bowl rings.

6

Super Bowl XXV: Norwood Misses a Field Goal

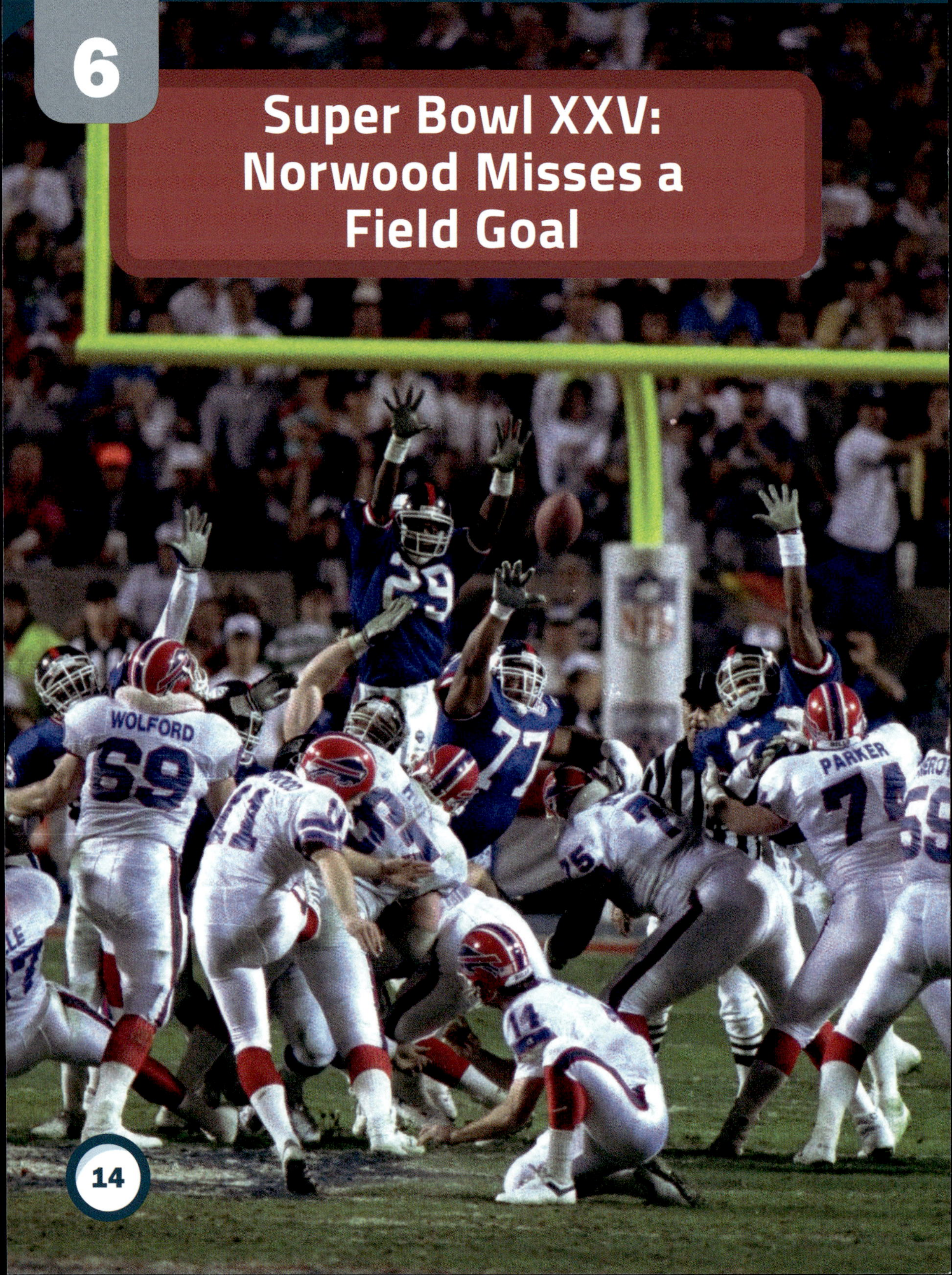

In 1991, Scott Norwood faced a situation that no other kicker had faced in a Super Bowl game.

The Buffalo Bills trailed the New York Giants by a single point in Super Bowl XXV. Norwood was called on for a field goal attempt of 47 yards. It was the last play of the game. A Norwood field goal would have given the Bills their first Super Bowl championship.

The kick went right of the goalposts. Norwood watched as the ball missed its mark. He walked off the field alone. New York Giants coach Bill Parcells threw his arms into the air. The kick became known in Super Bowl history as the "wide right" kick.

Other kickers became Super Bowl heroes. Adam Vinatieri won Super Bowls for the New England Patriots with field goals. A field goal by Jim O'Brien gave the Baltimore Colts a win in Super Bowl V. The kick by Norwood came in a different setting. The score was tied when Vinatieri and O'Brien won games. The Bills were trailing by one point when Norwood made his kick.

THINK ABOUT IT

What would you have said to Scott Norwood before he ran out to the field to attempt his kick? How would you have encouraged him?

2

Number of Super Bowls played by Buffalo Bills kicker Scott Norwood.

- Norwood missed a field goal of 47 yards on the last play of Super Bowl XXV. The miss became known as the "wide right" kick.
- The New York Giants held on for a victory over the Buffalo Bills by a score of 20 to 19.
- The game was the first of four consecutive losses by the Bills in Super Bowls.

7

Super Bowl XXXIV: Jones Saves the Game

Mike Jones perhaps made the biggest tackle in Super Bowl history. Jones was a linebacker for the St. Louis Rams. The year was 2000. The Tennessee Titans had the ball at the Rams 10-yard line with six seconds left in Super Bowl XXXIV. The Rams were ahead by a score of 23 to 16. The Titans had one last chance.

Titans quarterback Steve McNair threw a quick slant pass to Kevin Dyson. Dyson caught the ball. He headed for the end zone. Jones threw his arms around the legs of Dyson. He brought Dyson to the ground. Dyson tried to reach the football to the goal line. But he was short by about one yard. The St. Louis Rams won the game as a result.

It was the first Super Bowl game in Tennessee Titans history. It was also the first Super Bowl victory for the Rams. Quarterback Kurt Warner of the Rams was named game MVP. He passed for 414 yards and two touchdowns. The 414 passing yards were a Super Bowl record.

But the biggest play was clearly the tackle by Jones. He was an undrafted linebacker who began his NFL career in 1991 with the Raiders. He became a regular starter for the Rams in 1997. He played four seasons in St. Louis.

17

Number of seasons that Mike Jones played in the NFL. He played in one Super Bowl.

- In Super Bowl XXXIV, Mike Jones tackled Tennessee receiver Kevin Dyson just before he reached the end zone.
- Jones made the tackle on the last play. It won the game for the St. Louis Rams.
- The win was the first Super Bowl title for the Rams.

8

Super Bowl XXXVI: Vinatieri Kicks a Winning Field Goal

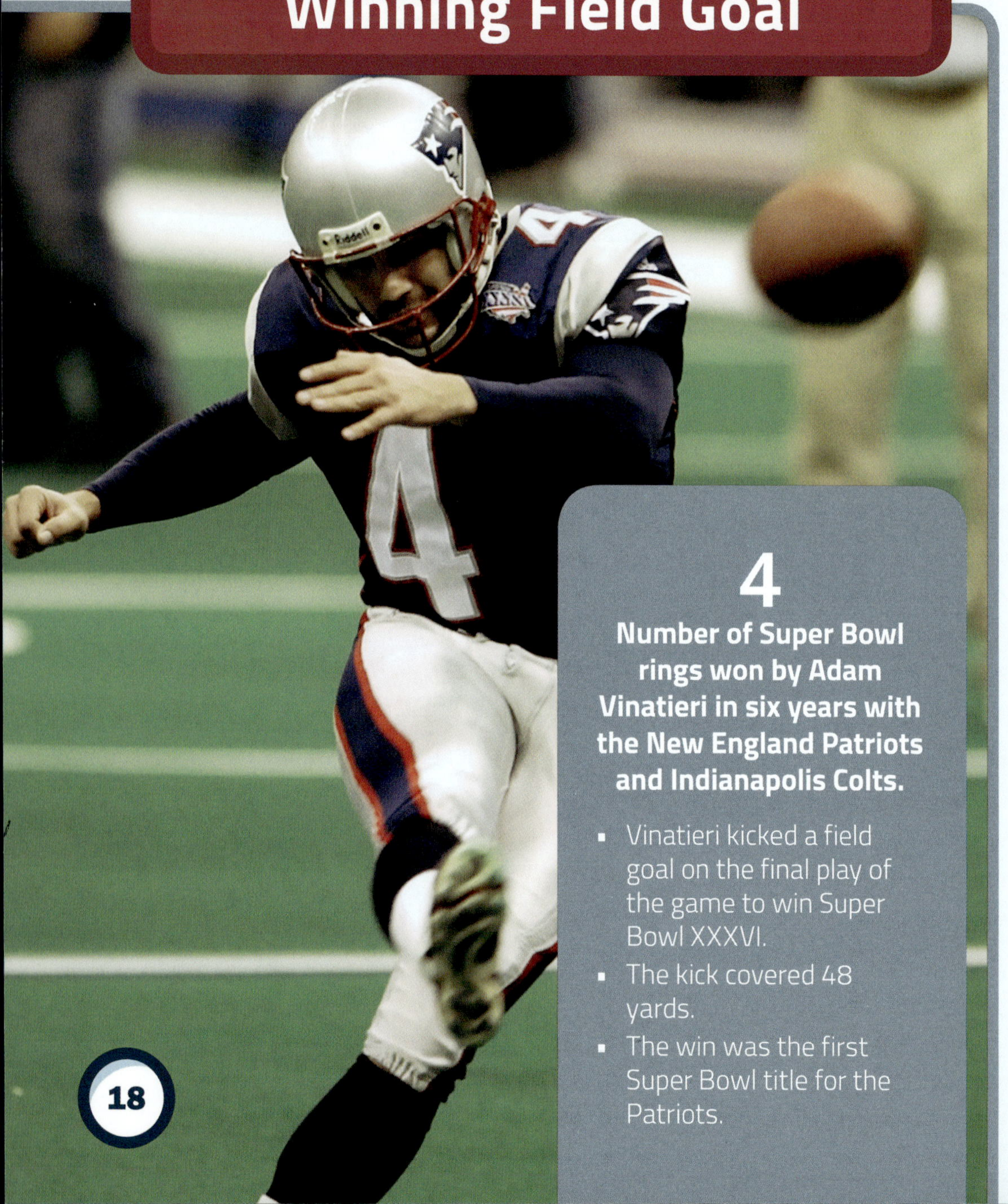

4

Number of Super Bowl rings won by Adam Vinatieri in six years with the New England Patriots and Indianapolis Colts.

- Vinatieri kicked a field goal on the final play of the game to win Super Bowl XXXVI.
- The kick covered 48 yards.
- The win was the first Super Bowl title for the Patriots.

Adam Vinatieri made history in Super Bowl XXXVI. The New England Patriots were trying to win their first Super Bowl in the 2002 championship game.

Patriots quarterback Tom Brady was playing in his first Super Bowl game. And so was Vinatieri. He was the Patriots placekicker. The Patriots and St. Louis Rams were tied with a score of 17 to 17. Brady led the Patriots down the field quickly. The Patriots began the drive at their own 17-yard line with 81 seconds left in the game.

Brady led the Patriots into Rams territory. He set the stage for Vinatieri. Vinatieri faced a field goal of 48 yards with seven seconds remaining. The snap came from center Lonie Paxton. Ken Walter was the holder. Everything was going perfectly. Vinatieri swung his right foot into the ball. It soared into the air. It went right through the goalposts. The Patriots won their first Super Bowl against the St. Louis Rams 20 to 17.

FOUR RINGS

Adam Vinatieri was the first placekicker to play in five Super Bowl games. He was also the first kicker to win four Super Bowl championships. He won Super Bowl XXXVI and Super Bowl XXXVIII for the New England Patriots with field goals. He also won Super Bowl XXXIX with the Patriots and Super Bowl XLI with the Indianapolis Colts. His seven field goals in five Super Bowl games set a Super Bowl record. His 13 extra points in those games also set a Super Bowl record.

9

Super Bowl XLII: Tyree Makes a Helmet Catch

The New York Giants were down to one of their last plays in Super Bowl XLII. The year was 2008. They trailed the New England Patriots by a score of 14 to 10. They were facing a third down play at their own 44-yard line. Just one minute and 16 seconds remained in the game. Giants quarterback Eli Manning dropped back to pass. The Patriots put defensive pressure on him. Manning tossed up a desperation pass to David Tyree. Tyree jumped for the ball and somehow pinned the ball against his helmet with his hands. He fell to the ground. He kept hold of the ball.

The play gave the Giants a first down. It was a pass play covering 32 yards. The Giants scored a touchdown four plays later. Plaxico Burress caught a scoring pass from Manning with 35 seconds left. The Giants won the game by a score of 17 to 14. The Patriots lost for the first time all season.

The helmet catch became known as one of the best catches in Super Bowl history. It was also the last catch Tyree had in the NFL.

THINK ABOUT IT

The helmet catch by Mike Tyree was one of the biggest catches in Super Bowl history. It was also one of the toughest to make. Is that a catch that you believe you would make? How would you keep the ball pinned against your helmet without dropping the ball?

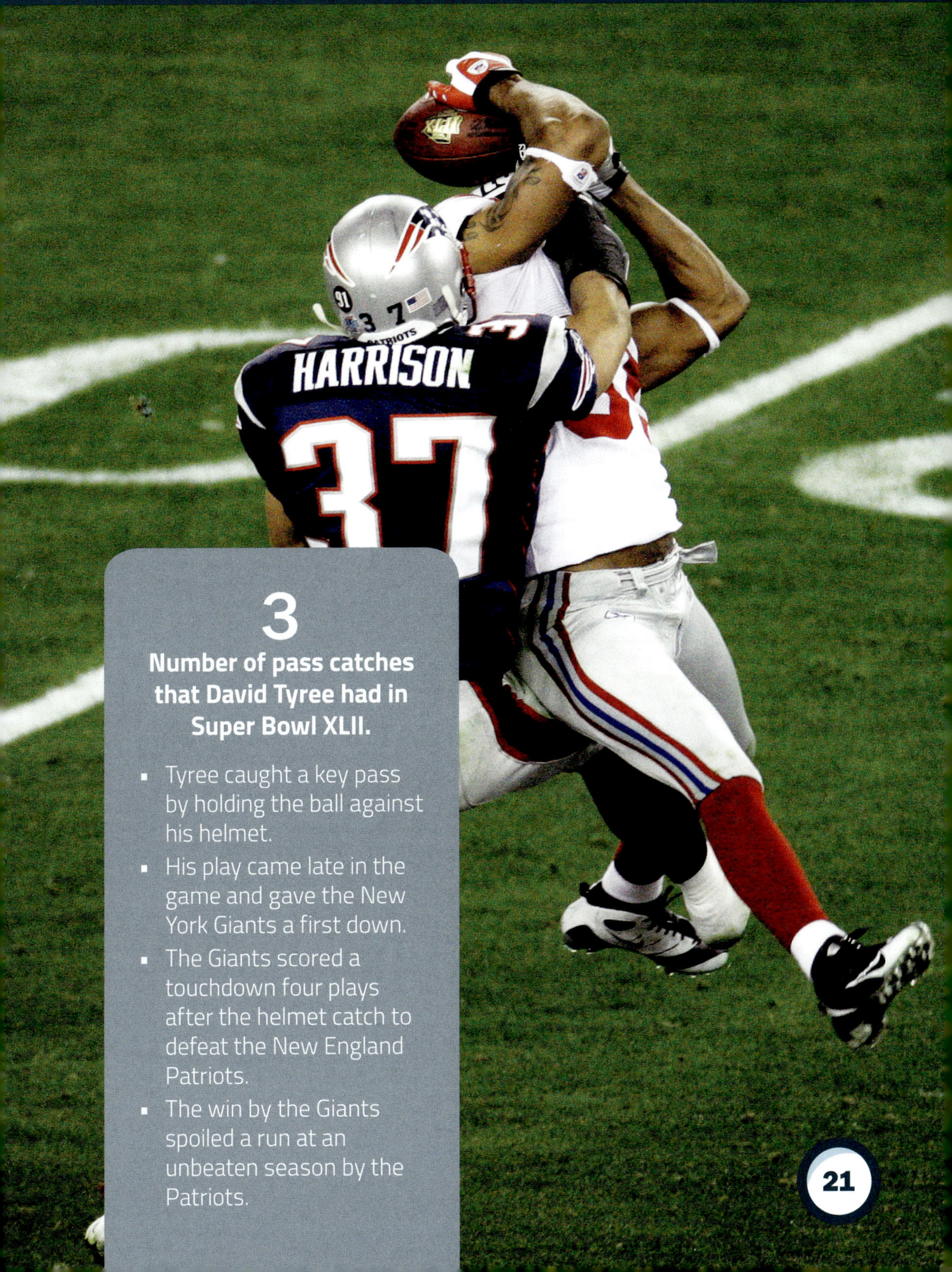

3

Number of pass catches that David Tyree had in Super Bowl XLII.

- Tyree caught a key pass by holding the ball against his helmet.
- His play came late in the game and gave the New York Giants a first down.
- The Giants scored a touchdown four plays after the helmet catch to defeat the New England Patriots.
- The win by the Giants spoiled a run at an unbeaten season by the Patriots.

10 Super Bowl XLIII: Holmes Scores on His Tiptoes

A tiptoe grab by Santonio Holmes lives on as perhaps the greatest touchdown catch in the history of the Pittsburgh Steelers. In 2009, they were going for their sixth Super Bowl win. The Steelers trailed the Arizona Cardinals in the final minute of Super Bowl XLIII.

Steelers quarterback Ben Roethlisberger lofted a pass over three Arizona defenders in the end zone. The ball came down toward Steelers receiver Santonio Holmes. He was in the corner of the end zone. He jumped up for the catch. He kept his toes inbounds. And then he fell out of bounds.

The play was ruled a touchdown because Holmes kept his toes inbounds. It gave the Steelers the lead with 35 seconds left. The Steelers won the game by a score of 27 to 23. Holmes was named Super Bowl MVP. He had a remarkable winning drive for the Steelers. He had four catches covering a total of 73 yards. The touchdown-catch covered six yards.

One of the key passes came two plays before the touchdown catch. Holmes caught a ball from Roethlisberger and raced 40 yards to the Cardinals 6-yard line. Holmes led all receivers in the game with nine catches for 131 yards.

131

Receiving yardage of Santonio Holmes in Super Bowl XLIII for the Pittsburgh Steelers.

- Holmes caught a touchdown pass on his tiptoes with 35 seconds left to win the game for the Steelers.
- He caught four passes on the game-winning drive and was named Super Bowl MVP.
- Holmes led all receivers with nine pass catches.
- It was the only Super Bowl game Holmes played in.

11

Super Bowl XLIII: Harrison Runs the Longest Play

The Arizona Cardinals trailed the Pittsburgh Steelers by just three points. It was Super Bowl XLIII in 2009. It was late in the first half. The Cardinals were on the Steelers 1-yard line. They were threatening to score. James Harrison of the Steelers made sure they didn't. Harrison intercepted a pass thrown by Cardinals quarterback Kurt Warner. Harrison stepped in front of Arizona receiver Anquan Boldin at the goal line. Harrison returned the interception 100 yards for a touchdown. It was the longest play in Super Bowl history.

Harrison was exhausted by the time he scored the touchdown 100 yards later. He dropped to the ground on his back. He was given oxygen through a mask to catch his breath. The touchdown put the Steelers ahead by 10 points. They defeated the Cardinals by a score of 27 to 23.

PLAYS TO REMEMBER

James Harrison broke the Super Bowl record by one yard. It was when he returned an interception 100 yards for a touchdown in Super Bowl XLIII. Desmond Howard of Green Bay returned a kickoff 99 yards for a touchdown in Super Bowl XXXI. Jacoby Jones of the Baltimore Ravens broke the record in Super Bowl XLVII. He returned a kickoff 108 yards for a touchdown.

3

Number of Super Bowls that James Harrison played with the Pittsburgh Steelers.

- Harrison returned an interception 100 yards for a touchdown in Super Bowl XLIII.
- It was the longest play in Super Bowl history.
- Harrison prevented an Arizona touchdown with the interception.

12

Super Bowl XLIX: Butler Intercepts in Last Minute of Game

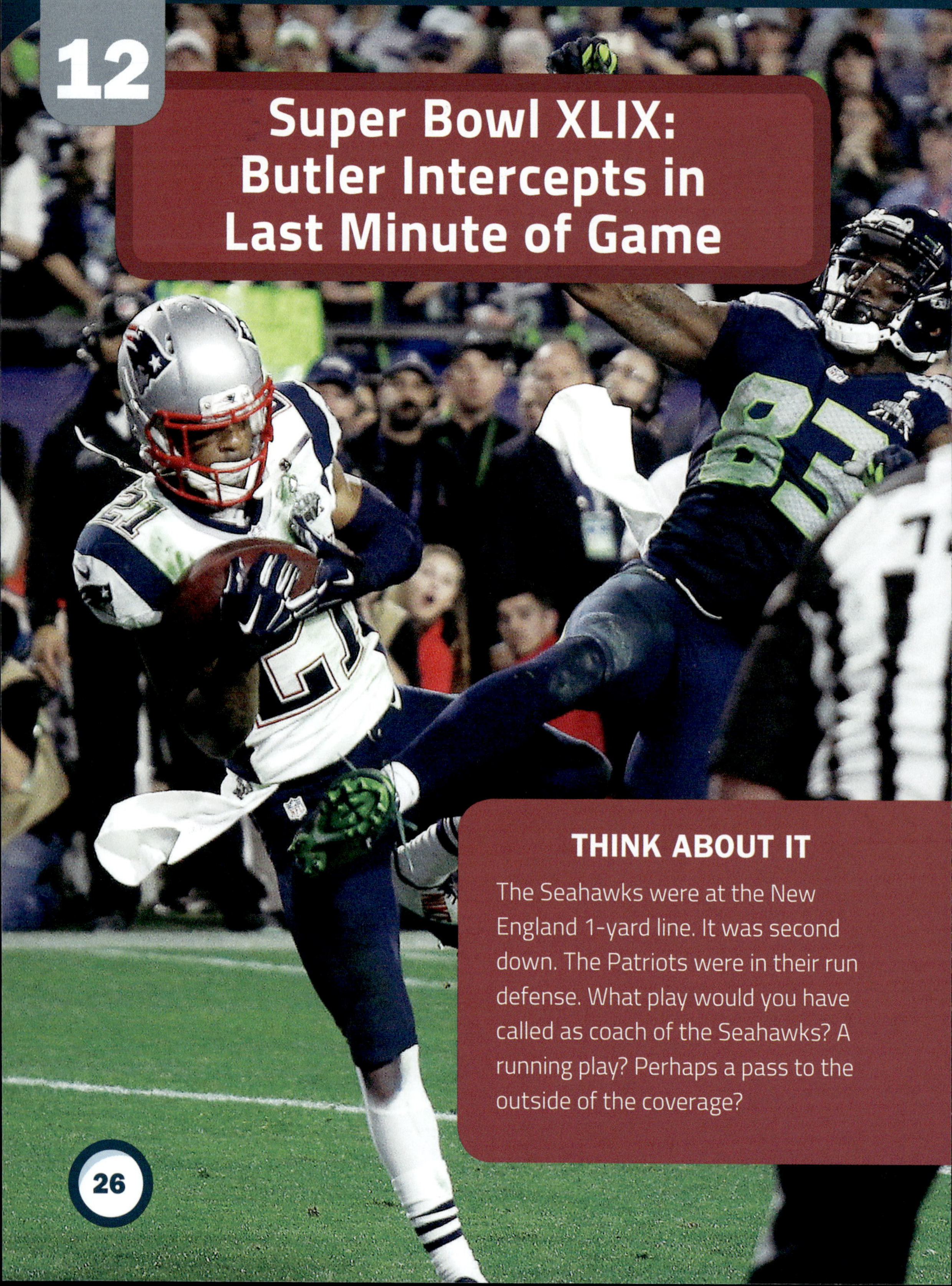

THINK ABOUT IT

The Seahawks were at the New England 1-yard line. It was second down. The Patriots were in their run defense. What play would you have called as coach of the Seahawks? A running play? Perhaps a pass to the outside of the coverage?

It was 2015. The Seattle Seahawks appeared to be closing in on a victory in Super Bowl XLIX.

The Seahawks trailed the New England Patriots by four points. They had the ball at the 1-yard line of New England. It was just second down. Malcolm Butler of the Patriots then lunged into Super Bowl history.

The Patriots were in a goal-line defense and expecting a run. The Seahawks called a pass play instead of a run. Butler jumped a slant pass route. He intercepted a pass thrown by Seahawks quarterback Russell Wilson. The pass was intended for Ricardo Lockette. The defensive play of the game came with 26 seconds left. It gave the Patriots the ball and the victory. The Patriots won the game by a score of 28 to 24.

Butler became an immediate Super Bowl hero. The Super Bowl finished up his rookie year in which he started just one game. Butler went on to win another Super Bowl ring with the Patriots in 2017.

1

Number of interceptions by Malcom Butler in his Super Bowl XLIX debut.

- Butler intercepted a pass on the goal line in the final minute of Super Bowl XLIX.
- The interception saved a victory for the New England Patriots against the Seattle Seahawks.
- Butler won two Super Bowls with the New England Patriots.

Fun Facts and Stories

Parking Pass Problem

Marcus Allen was the star of Super Bowl XVIII. His touchdown run of 74 yards set a Super Bowl record. His rushing total of 191 yards also set a record. He led the Los Angeles Raiders to a Super Bowl win over the Washington Redskins. Allen was named MVP. Getting to the game was another story. Allen was denied access to the stadium parking lot in Tampa, Florida. He didn't have a parking pass. So he stopped the car at the curb. He got out. He grabbed his bag and ran to the stadium.

Candy Man

The San Francisco 49ers were down by three points in the final quarter of Super Bowl XXIII. They were at their own 8-yard line. Quarterback Joe Montana chose to lighten up the mood in the team huddle. He looked into the crowd and mentioned to his teammates that he saw actor John Candy. The players smiled. The tension had been broken. And the 49ers went on to defeat the Cincinnati Bengals in the final minute.

Linked Forever

Mike Jones of the St. Louis Rams tackled Kevin Dyson of the Tennessee Titans one yard short of the end zone. It ended Super Bowl XXXIV. The Rams won the game. Years later Jones and Dyson watched the play together at the high school where Dyson works. Every year they talk on the phone about the play. Jones says they will be connected by that play for the rest of their lives.

Retirement Day

Super Bowl XLIII MVP Santonio Holmes was a Chicago Bear in his final season in the NFL. But he was a famed star for the Pittsburgh Steelers. He won Super Bowl XLIII with a tip-toe catch in the final minute of the game. His final year in the NFL was in 2014 with the Bears. Three years later he officially retired as a member of the Pittsburgh Steelers. It was important for Holmes to have his legacy as a Steeler remembered.

Taking His Breath Away

James Harrison lost his breath after returning an interception in Super Bowl XLIII. It was the longest play in Super Bowl history at that point. He returned the interception 100 yards for a touchdown. He dropped to the ground on his back after the play. He did not move for at least a couple of minutes. He received oxygen through a mask. He was then helped to his feet as the referee officially announced it was a touchdown.

Glossary

goal line
A line located at the beginning of each end zone. If a player with the ball crosses the goal line, they score a touchdown.

goalposts
Two vertical posts placed above the goal line. A kicker must kick the ball between the goalposts and above the crossbar in order to score.

Hall of Fame
An organization that recognizes outstanding players. A player is eligible to be voted into the Hall of Fame after finishing their career.

interception
When a pass is caught by a player from the opposing team.

linebacker
A defensive player who is positioned behind the scrimmage line. They make tackles on both running and short passing plays.

line of scrimmage
A line on the field where the ball is placed before a play begins.

MVP
Abbreviation for most valuable player.

quarterback
A quarterback is the player who runs the offense. They take the ball on a snap from the center. The quarterback usually passes the ball or hands it off to a running back.

running back
A player who lines up in the backfield with the quarterback. Their job is to receive the ball from the quarterback and run with it. Or they may also catch a pass or block for another player who has the ball.

slant route
A pass route run by a receiver. The receiver crosses the field at a slant so the quarterback can throw the ball to them in front of defenders from the other team.

touchdown
When a player with the ball gets into the end zone. A touchdown scores six points.

For More Information

Books

Morey, Allan, *The Pittsburgh Steelers Story:* Bellwether Media, 2016.

Mack, Larry, *The Washington Redskins Story:* Bellwether Media, 2016.

Nelson, Julie, *New York Giants, Mankato,* MN: NFL Today, Creative Education, 2001.

Index

About the Author

Paul Bowker is an editor and author who lives on Cape Cod in South Yarmouth, Massachusetts. His 35-year newspaper career has included hundreds of NFL games. He is a national past president of Associated Press Sports Editors and has won multiple national writing awards.